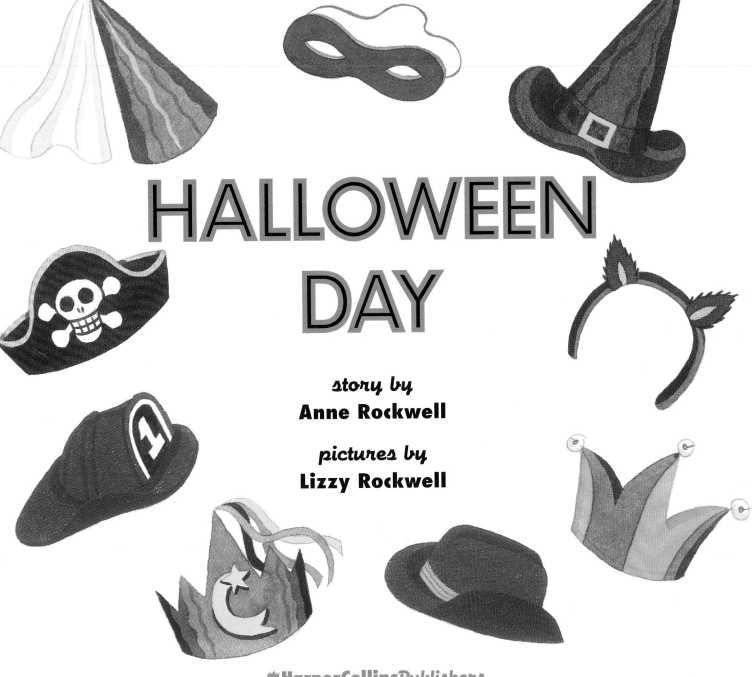

HALLOWEEN DAY

story by
Anne Rockwell

pictures by
Lizzy Rockwell

HarperCollinsPublishers

Halloween Day Text copyright © 1997 by Anne Rockwell Illustrations copyright © 1997 by Lizzy Rockwell Printed in the U.S.A. All rights reserved. Library of Congress Cataloging-in-Publication Data Rockwell, Anne F. Halloween day / story by Anne Rockwell ; pictures by Lizzy Rockwell. p. cm. Summary: The ten preschoolers in Mrs. Madoff's class wear their Halloween costumes to school, filling the room with a cat, a pirate, a witch, and other characters. ISBN 0-06-027567-7. — ISBN 0-06-443589-X (pbk.) [1. Halloween—Fiction. 2. Costumes—Fiction. 3. Schools—Fiction.] I. Rockwell, Lizzy, ill. II. Title. PZ7.R5943Hal 1997 96-36680 [E]—dc20 CIP AC Typography by Elynn Cohen ❖ For more information, visit us at our web site at http://www.harperchildrens.com.

For Nigel

Today is going to be a very exciting day.
I'm going to wear my Halloween costume to school.
My friends will wear their costumes, too.

Wow—look at us!
Some of us look scary,
and some of us look beautiful.
But all of us look great.

I wonder where Mrs. Madoff is.
I want her to see my costume.
Maybe Mr. Siscoe will be our teacher
all by himself today.

I wish Mrs. Madoff could hear me say,
"Meee-owww!"
while I swish my long black tail.

The fierce pirate with the patch over his eye
and the red scar painted on his cheek
is really Nicholas.

Charlie looks just like
the real firefighters who work
in the firehouse on Main Street.

The witch wearing a tall
black hat is Kate.
She told me that was
what she was going to be.

Sarah showed us how cowpokes out West
twirl their lariats and sing,
"Yippee-eye-oh-kye-yay!"

Then Mr. Siscoe said it was time
for our Halloween parade.

A beautiful fairy godmother appeared in the hall.
Who could she be?

I'll bet the big orange pumpkin is really Pablo.
Yes, I'm sure it is.
Those look like Pablo's new sneakers.

If the big orange pumpkin is really Pablo,
then the boy in the gross green monster mask
must be Sam.
Yes—the pumpkin and the monster are
walking together just like Sam and Pablo
always do.

Eveline is pretending she's a clown.
She can turn somersaults
just like the clowns in the circus did.
She did one right in front of the library,
and everyone clapped.

Mr. Siscoe thought Evan was a robot,
but I knew right away that he was an astronaut.

Jessica is dressed up like Comet Queen on TV.
I think that program is scary.
But Jessica isn't scared of anything.

At snack time, we had a Halloween party.
Our fairy godmother waved her magic wand
over some orange tissue paper in a big box.
She said, "Abracadabra, cuppity-boo!
What do you think I have for you?"

OXIGIN

Suddenly the box was full of cupcakes—
one for each of us!
Mr. Siscoe gave us candy corn and apple cider, too.

I ate my candy corn and drank my cider,
but I saved my cupcake for last
because I liked looking at its funny pumpkin face.

Guess what!?
Mrs. Madoff was with us all the time!
She was pretending to be our fairy godmother
for Halloween.